The Submarine Pitch

The Submarine Pitch

by Matt Christopher

Illustrated by Marcy Ramsey

Little, Brown and Company
Boston Toronto London

First Paperback Edition

Library of Congress Cataloging-in-Publication Data

Christopher, Matthew F.
The submarine pitch.

SUMMARY: When he learns why his best friend taught him an unbeatable pitch instead of using it himself, Bernie learns a sad lesson about friendship.
ISBN 0-316-13969-6 (hc)
ISBN 0-316-14250-6 (pb)
[1. Baseball — Fiction. 2. Friendship — Fiction.]
I. Title.
PZ7.C458Su [Fic] 75-25790

10 9 8 7 6 5 4 3 2 1

MV-NY

Published simultaneously in Canada
by Little, Brown & Company (Canada) Limited

Printed in the United States of America

THE SUBMARINE PITCH

1

THERE WAS NO WAY in the world that Bernie Shantz would have connected a lady's vanity with baseball. A vanity was a piece of furniture with drawers into which women put their personal things, such as cosmetics. Baseball was — well, everybody knew what baseball was.

Actually, what brought about the connection was the newspaper clipping that AnnMarie found in the bottom drawer of the vanity. How it got there, whose it was, and why it was there were the questions that immediately bothered Bernie, Ann-Marie, his fifteen-year-old sister, who had bought it from a friend, and Frankie, the youngest of the Shantz clan.

"Hey, read this," said Frankie, who was only eight and longed to be old enough to play ball on his brother's team.

"It's about a guy who used to pitch for a team called the Keystones," said Ann-Marie, who looked up at Bernie with her enormous blue eyes.

"He threw a submarine pitch," Frankie added. "Ever hear of a submarine pitch? Weird, ain't it?"

Bernie frowned as he looked at his sister and brother. "Submarine pitch? No."

"It must've been some pitch," said Frankie, looking at his brother anxiously. "It says here that he had the strikeout record in the league for three years."

Bernie knew why Frankie had that anxious look on his face. Bernie was a pitcher himself. Was — until last week, that is. Since then he had given it up, closed it out of his life forever. No more pitching. In fact, no more baseball *at all* for him, except watching it on the tube, maybe. He just wasn't cut out for it, no matter how much he loved it. He knew his decision bothered Frankie, who couldn't understand why his older brother didn't want to play ball anymore. Well, Frankie was just a kid. He wouldn't.

"Dusty Fowler," Bernie began to read out loud, "pitching his fourth straight victory of the season against Rockville in the City Twilight League, says of his pitching form, 'I throw that way because it's the easiest for me. I can throw all day if I have to and not get tired. The thing is, I can't throw overhand if I try. I hurt my shoulder one day while baling hay, and I've been throwing underhand ever since.' "

There was more, but Bernie didn't care to read any further.

"You'd better give this back to the people you bought the vanity from," he said to AnnMarie. "They might not have known it was there and would want it back."

"But their name isn't Fowler," Frankie intervened. "It's Hudson. Why would *they* want it back?"

Bernie looked at him. "Dusty Fowler could've been a friend," he replied. "Anyway," he turned to AnnMarie, "I think you should call the Hudsons and tell them about it."

"But," said Frankie, not one to yield so easily, "there's more about that submarine pitch that I think you should know."

"I don't care." Bernie's eyes flashed as he looked at his younger brother. "I know what you're thinking, Frankie, and you might as well get it out of your head. I'm through with baseball. Through . . . finished . . . out. Okay?"

Frankie looked at him with large eyes. Bernie paused. No kid on the block read as much about baseball players and teams as Frankie did. When it came to records, Frankie was a walking encyclopedia. And Bernie – although he wouldn't say so – admired him for it.

"Okay," said Frankie. "I just thought . . ." He turned and went out of the room abruptly without finishing what he was going to say.

AnnMarie took the clipping from Bernie. "Too bad he's too young to play," she said icily. "I think he's really more nuts about baseball than you are."

"Yeah, I know," said Bernie sullenly.

There was a sound from the other room, and then a cheery greeting, as a boy with rust-colored hair and a thin smattering of freckles on his high-cheekboned face came in.

"Hi, AnnMarie. Hi, Bernie. What's new?"

"Hi, Dave," AnnMarie greeted him. "Heard you were in New York?"

Dave Grant smiled. "I was. But that was just over Sunday to see the Mets game. Dad had to be back to work today." He looked at the clipping in AnnMarie's hand. "Hey, that looks like something out of an old newspaper. Anything important?"

"It's a clipping I found in a drawer of a vanity I just bought," AnnMarie explained. "I was about to call up the woman

I bought it from and ask her if she wants it back. Maybe it dropped out of her husband's scrapbook. Excuse me."

As she started out of the room Bernie saw Dave open his mouth as if he were going to call to her, but then he closed it and looked at Bernie. A sheepish grin came over his face.

"Hey, man," he said. "That was quite a game I saw. I hope you can come with us sometime."

Dave's acting kind of peculiar. Does he have a secret with AnnMarie? thought Bernie.

"I might, sometime," he answered, frowning. Ever since the major league baseball season had opened, Dave and his father had gone to New York City to see games. They had gone to Syracuse to see International League games, too. Ap parently Mr. Grant enjoyed baseball as much as his son did, although he seldom talked about it in Bernie's presence.

Bernie studied Dave's face; his friend's warm blue eyes looked restless. Something seemed to be bothering Dave, that was sure.

Dave lived four blocks away and he was Bernie's best friend. They were in the same grade at Lake Center School and shared similar interests: fossil collecting, weird comic books, and horror movies.

"You in trouble?" Bernie asked. After being friends for two years, you can tell when something's bothering a guy.

Dave shook his head. "Trouble? No. Why?" His phony smile made Bernie even more suspicious.

Bernie shrugged. "I don't know. You kind of look as if something's bothering you."

Dave forced a chuckle. Bernie was pretty sure now that he was right — something *was* bothering Dave. Well, maybe it was something personal. Something Dave didn't want to tell him about.

In a minute AnnMarie came back into the room, Frankie close behind her.

"Know what?" she said casually. "Mrs. Hudson doesn't know a thing about this clipping."

Bernie looked at her. If Mrs. Hudson didn't know a thing about the clipping, how could it have gotten into the vanity?

"Well," AnnMarie said, "I won't have to return it, so that saves a trip over to Douglas Street."

Hardly were the words out of her mouth when she turned toward Dave. Her blue eyes fastened on him.

"Dave, you must know the Hudsons," she said. "They're your neighbors."

He blushed and then nodded. "Yeah, that's right," he said. "They live four doors from us."

Bernie suddenly got an idea about the clipping's origin. He poked a finger gently into Dave's ribs. "Buddy boy," he said, "is there an itty-bitty chance that *you* know how that clipping got into Mrs. Hudson's vanity?"

The smile flickered on Dave's face. "I guess it's no use for me to keep my mouth shut any longer, is it?"

Bernie shook his head. "No, it isn't. I thought you were acting kind of funny. I read that clipping, Dave. A part of it, anyway. It won't work. Frankie's been trying to get me back into pitching, too. I won't do it. I'm through."

"But you didn't read the *whole* clipping, Bernie," said Frankie from the doorway.

"You didn't come to the most important part."

Bernie looked at him. "Most important part? What was that?"

"About the pitch," replied Frankie, stepping forward as if he were glad for the chance to participate in the conversation. "There's something about that submarine pitch that's really weird."

"Oh?" Bernie's eyebrows went up a notch. "What do you mean? How can a pitch be weird?"

AnnMarie handed him back the clipping. "Here," she said. "Maybe you'll learn more about it by reading the whole thing this time."

Curious, Bernie took the clipping from her and started to read it again from the beginning. By the time he was finished with it, his skin was prickling.

2

THE PITCH COMES UP like a submarine coming up out of the water, which is how it got its name," Bernie read. "It sails in a straight path toward the plate, rising all the time until it reaches the batter. Then, at the last instant, the ball curves sharply — away from a right-handed batter, toward a left-handed batter.

"Some batters have accused Dusty of putting some kind of substance on the ball, such as saliva, to make it act the way it does. But no evidence has been found that such is the case. He just throws the ball naturally, and it comes up to the batter, curves, and then flies by into the catcher's mitt. The batter either watches it go by or swings at it, usually missing it by a foot. If Dusty Fowler keeps his pitch under control, no one will be the least surprised to hear that some major league ball club has signed him up."

Bernie waited for his pulse to slow down a bit. He had read about pitchers throwing the illegal spitball in the big leagues, but never had he heard of *any-one* throwing a submarine pitch.

"Does this clipping belong to you or your father?" Bernie asked.

"It's my father's," admitted Dave. "I got it out of his scrapbook of interesting sports stories. When I saw the guys loading the piece of furniture on the truck and they said that they were bringing it over here to your house, I got it and stuck it into the bottom drawer. I suppose it was a stupid thing to do."

"Not stupid, just silly," said Bernie. "Did this guy, Dusty Fowler, ever make it to the big leagues?"

"No. He only got as far as the International. But that wasn't bad."

"Why don't you try it, Bernie?" Frankie broke in with that soft, eager voice of his that had a way of grabbing Bernie's attention.

"Try what?" said Bernie.

"Learn to throw that submarine pitch," Frankie answered. "You said yourself that your overhand pitches are like fat balloons to the batters. Maybe if you learn this submarine pitch you won't have to give up baseball."

Frankie made it sound so simple. Ann-

Marie had said that he probably loved baseball more than Bernie did. Well, that wasn't true. No one could love it more than Bernie did. He was just too darned proud, that was his trouble. He wanted to be really good at it, and he just couldn't be.

Last year he had tried pitching because he had a fair throwing arm. He had no curve, but his overhand delivery could cut the plate in two most of the time. His problem was not being able to get the ball past the hitters. Players on the other teams always hoped Bernie would be pitching to them. They boosted their batting averages every time he pitched for the Rangers.

In the infield or outfield he was no worse than any other fielder; his troubles all centered around the plate. For when he was up pitchers were as happy to see him bat as batters were to see him pitch. He couldn't hit, and whoever heard of a nonhitting fielder?

Why should he make a fool of himself again this year?

"I've brought a ball and mitt," said Dave. "Get your glove and let's throw a few. Maybe you can develop into another Dusty Fowler."

"Yeah, Bernie! Let's!" cried Frankie. His eyes flashed as if it were he about whom all the fuss was being made.

Bernie glanced at AnnMarie, not saying anything, but asking her with his eyes if what Dave was asking him to do made sense.

As if she read his thoughts she said, "You know how nuts you are about baseball, Bernie. I was just kidding you when I said that Frankie loves it more than you do. If you don't play, you'll mope around here all summer and bug both Mom and me out of our minds. I think you ought to listen to Dave."

"Come on!" Dave insisted, and started out of the house. "You're not doing anything else right now, anyway."

Reluctantly, Bernie got his glove and ball and went out to the backyard with Dave. If it were anyone else but Dave who tried to coax him, he would definitely refuse. But he'd do it for Dave – mainly to satisfy Dave, not himself.

He threw his first pitch, not concentrating on whether it was overhand or underhand.

"Underhand," reminded Dave. "Throw it underhand. Like this."

Thinking that *no one* he knew threw underhand, Dave threw the ball back to

him, bringing it up from the side of his body, near his knees. The ball streaked up to Bernie and then, just as it got near him, it curved inward, toward Bernie's right side.

"Hey, did you see that?" Bernie exclaimed. "It hooked!"

"That's what it's supposed to do," said Dave, proudly. "It comes naturally if you throw it right."

"Maybe *you* should pitch for the Rangers," suggested Bernie.

"No chance. But I wish I could," replied Dave.

Bernie felt slightly embarrassed because he remembered that Dave had said recently that he might never be able to play baseball again. He used to, but last spring he had gotten sick and hadn't played since. His participation now was limited to easy games of pitch and catch.

Bernie started to throw the ball underhand, bringing it up from his knees as Dave had done. At first the pitch was slightly wild, forcing Dave to leap out after it. But each successive throw got better, and before long, Bernie had the pitch fairly well under control.

"Hey, man!" Dave cried. "You're doing fine!"

Bernie grinned. "You make a lousy liar, you know that?"

Frankie sprawled on his stomach, watching them play. "Look who's here," he said a few minutes later.

Bernie paused and looked toward the street. Two guys who played with the Sharks were coming up to the fence separating the sidewalk from the yard. The taller of them, the light-haired one wearing a white T-shirt, was Vincent Steele, the Sharks' cleanup hitter. The other was Mick Devlan, the Sharks' catcher.

"Hold it," said Dave, and looked at his wristwatch. "It's almost five. I've got to beat it."

He went up to Bernie, catching a soft throw and squeezing the mitt around it. "Don't breathe a word about the submarine pitch to those guys or to anybody else," he said under his breath. "Let's keep it between us. Okay?"

He was breathing unusually hard, as if they'd been playing for hours.

"Okay. Are you all right, Dave?"

"Yes, I'm okay. Just a little tired. See you."

Dave left, waving to the two newcomers as he walked out of the yard and across the street. Bernie watched him. *Maybe someday he'll tell me what is really ailing him*, he thought.

"Heard that you're not going to pitch for the Rangers this year, Bernie," said Vincent. "What's the beef?"

"I'm holding out for more money," said Bernie.

Both Vincent and Mick laughed. "What did your coach do? Promise to pay you for not playing?" said Vincent.

"Just wait'll the season opens," Frankie piped up. "We'll see who'll be laughing then."

"Is that so?" said Mick. "Well, well, well! How about that, Vince? Did you hear the kid?"

"I heard some noise," replied Vince, looking around and then back at Bernie, a pretended look of puzzlement on his face.

Bernie stared coldly at Frankie. He didn't say a word, but he didn't have to. Frankie had learned a long time ago what the looks that his older brother gave him under varying circumstances meant.

"If you guys don't mind, we've got to go in," said Bernie. "See you around."

"Sure," said Vincent, and he and Mick took off down the sidewalk.

Frankie rose to his feet and came trotting up beside Bernie. "I'm sorry, Bernie," he said, his eyes wide and apologetic. "I shouldn't have said what I did, should I?"

"No, you shouldn't," said Bernie, still smoldering. "For a little kid you've got a big mouth, you know that?"

Frankie's jaw slacked. He turned away, his eyes blinking.

"I'm sorry," said Bernie, reaching out toward his brother. "You were sticking up for me and didn't think what you were saying, but Dave did ask us not to talk about the pitch."

He put his arm around Frankie's shoulders and squeezed him gently as they walked to the house. As long as he could remember, Frankie had always looked up to him as an older, wiser brother. Quite often Frankie had gone to him for advice about something — such as fixing his bike chain when a link had broken — instead of going to Dad. He liked the feeling. Frankie was more than a brother. He was a pal.

And now his brother and his best friend wanted him to learn this new "wonder" pitch. He felt a creepy sensation shooting through him as he remembered Dave's pitches to him. Each one had hooked as it came over the plate.

His didn't. They were always straight as a string. But *maybe* in time the submarine pitch would work for him.

3

"ONE THIRTY-NINE . . . ONE FORTY . . . ONE FORTY-ONE . . ."

Bernie heard a light knock on the door, then the door opening and finally closing.

He kept on counting. ". . . one forty-two . . . one forty-three . . . one forty-four."

That was it. One hundred forty-four dollars. He folded up the bills and pushed them into the canvas bag Dad had picked up for him at the bank.

"Wow! That's quite a pile of moola, Bernie," said Frankie. "Haven't you saved up enough yet for that bike?"

Bernie opened a drawer and dropped the bag of money into it. Then he turned around and faced Frankie, who had plunked himself down on his bed. The brothers shared the room. Each had his own desk and his own preferred team pennants and sports prints on the wall nearest his bed.

"No," Bernie answered, stretching out his bare legs and wiggling his toes. "I've got a lot more to earn yet."

Frankie whistled. "Man! I didn't think mountain bikes cost that much!"

"Well, they do," said Bernie. "That means a lot of lawn mowing and small jobs I've got to scratch up. Maybe I won't have time to go out for baseball after all."

Frankie's head jerked up off the bed as if he'd been stung. He looked at Bernie with disbelieving eyes. "Won't have time for baseball?" he echoed. "Don't say that,

Bernie! With that submarine pitch you might turn out to be the best pitcher in the league!"

"That's crazy, Frankie," said Bernie. "You saw how many pitches I threw to Dave yesterday. Not one curved as much as a hair. I might as well keep throwing overhand and watch the pitches being knocked all over the lot."

"It will, though," Frankie insisted. "You just keep throwing it. You'll see."

Bernie shook his head. This kid was impossible. *Maybe what I need is some of his grit*, he thought.

Then he thought about Dave and about Dave's attitude when Vince and Mike had stopped by to watch them play catch.

"Frankie, did you notice how Dave acted when Vince and Mick showed up?" he said. "Right away he wanted to quit. He didn't want them to watch me throw that pitch. I think he *really* wants us to keep it a secret."

"Sure, he does," replied Frankie seriously. A smile curved his lips. "You know what? Sometimes he acts as if he's your brother, too."

Bernie nodded. "I know. That's why I — I hate to disappoint him."

For a week Bernie worked on the submarine pitch, practicing it either at his own home or at Dave's, and he had made solid improvement. There was a hook on the end of the pitch now. He had discovered how to accomplish it by twisting his wrist just slightly when releasing the ball.

He never worked out long at a time, though. About fifteen minutes was the limit, for Dave wanted to stop to rest then. But after half an hour's rest Dave would insist that they continue. This they did two or three times a day.

The only other time they paused for a rest was when a kid who played on an opposing team stopped by for a visit. This, too, was Dave's idea. He was really serious about not wanting anybody else to know about the submarine pitch.

"Why, Dave?" asked Bernie, when it happened for the third time. "Why don't you want anybody else to know about the pitch?"

Dave looked at him seriously, as if he couldn't understand why Bernie should ask him such a question.

"Because I want this to surprise them," he explained. "If you're going to start pitching when the league opens in a couple of weeks, you'd want the pitch developed enough to make it effective, wouldn't you?"

Bernie frowned at him. Dave sure was serious about the pitch, all right. He was talking as if he were Bernie's pitching coach. Well, in a way he was. He had introduced Bernie to the pitch, showed him how to throw it, and was having him practice it as often as he could. He was doing everything a pitching coach would do.

But Dave was taking a lot for granted, too.

"Dave, I haven't really said that I was going to pitch," said Bernie.

The statement seemed to hit Dave like a bombshell. "What do you mean you haven't said? I thought that's why we've been working on the submarine pitch all this time."

"I know. But it's real new for me, Dave. I might walk every guy that steps up to the plate."

"But you won't! Your control is good. Real good." Dave wiped a sleeve across his sweating forehead. "You can't say that you're not going to pitch, Bernie. You just *can't.*"

Bernie stared at him. "I don't get it, Dave," he said. "Why should you be so anxious that I pitch? I could see why my brother Frankie is. But why you?"

Dave gazed at him a long minute. "Because I can't do it myself," he answered finally. "Don't ask me why, but I can't. I would like to see you do it . . . for me."

"Suppose I fail?"

"That's all right. I'm not worried about that."

Again Bernie frowned, puzzled by Dave's answer.

"Okay, Dave," he said finally. "If you have faith in me, I should have, too. I'll give Coach Salerno a call tonight and ask him if he'll still have me for the Rangers."

Dave's face brightened. "You won't have to," he said.

"Why? What do you mean?"

"I've already talked with him," replied Dave. "He's got your name. And he wants you to be at the ball park Saturday morning for a practice game against the Atoms."

"Why, you stinker!" cried Bernie, poking him in the stomach.

"I knew you'd like that," said Dave, grinning.

The Atoms looked as if they had changed into their new uniforms in a sporting goods store; their white jerseys and blue pants were spanking clean. The Rangers' uniforms, green jerseys and white pants, were clean, too, but had that telltale look of having been through the mill. The fuzz was nearly all worn off all the pants at the knees, giving them a burlapish look.

Both teams had their names on the fronts of the jerseys and large numbers on the backs. Bernie's number was 3.

The catchers of both teams flipped a coin to see who'd bat first. Fritz Boon, the Atoms' catcher — a roly-poly kid who seemed to have been squeezed into his uniform — won the toss and chose to bat last.

"Okay, here's the roster," said Coach Salerno. He wasn't quite as stout as Fritz, nor as short, and his red, long-brimmed cap made him stand out like a cardinal among a flock of sparrows. He thumbtacked the list to the side of the dugout. "Read it to find out who you follow in the batting order and let's get started. Bernie, you're chucking."

Although Bernie expected it, hearing the coach tell him was like a slight electric shock. He nodded, and then felt suddenly numb as questions popped into his head. *Suppose I can't throw the ball within a mile of the plate? Suppose that even if I do get it over the Atoms blast it all over the lot?*

He shook the thoughts loose from his mind and went over to read the roster.

Bill Conley — shortstop
Ed Masters — right field
Deke Smith — first base
Buzz Ames — left field
Tom McDermott — second base
Rudy Sims — center field
Chuck Haley — third base
Fred Button — catcher
Bernie Shantz — pitcher

Chris Morgan, the Atoms' pitcher, had an overhand delivery that reminded Bernie very much of the way he used to throw. But Chris's pitches could thread a needle. Nearly all of them were teasers, thrown near or below the batters' knees. In the top of the first both Bill and Ed struck out and Deke grounded out to short.

The teams exchanged sides, and after a few warm-up pitches Bernie toed the rubber and winged in his first submarine pitch that anybody had ever seen besides Frankie and Dave.

A soft, surprised cry broke from the Atom bench.

"Hey! What kind of a pitch was that?" one of the guys exclaimed.

"I don't know. I've never seen him throw like that before," observed another.

Bernie got two balls and two strikes on

the leadoff batter, Ralph Benz — who stood in a deep crouch at the plate — then struck him out. As the infielders whipped the ball around the horn, Bernie felt his heart pound. One down, two to go.

Jim Hayes, the Atoms' second batter, waited out the pitches till the count built up to three and two. Then he too swung at a high sweeping pitch and whiffed.

Hank Dooley, the Atoms' left fielder, got a piece of the ball and beat out a scratch hit to third. Then Mark Pine, the Atoms' big gun, let two strikes go by him and swung at the third, missing it by a foot.

Bernie heard the hum rise among the Atom players as he walked off the mound. His heart was still pounding, though not as hard as before.

His own teammates showered him with words of praise. The coach shook his hand, grinning. "I don't know what you're throwing, kid," he said, "but whatever it is, don't lose it."

But the voice that he heard when he was near the dugout was the one that really mattered.

"What did I tell you, Bernie? Huh? What did I tell you?"

4

BUZZ AMES SINGLED to center, scooted to second on Tom's sacrifice bunt, and scored on Rudy's smashing drive through short. The Ranger bench yelled as if the 1–0 lead were the straw that would break the Atoms' back.

They picked up two more runs when Fred belted a double, scoring both Rudy and Chuck, who had walked on four straight pitches. Then Bernie popped out to second and Bill fanned to end the top half of the second inning. Rangers 3; Atoms 0.

Bernie's second time on the mound was

almost a replica of his first, except that he had only one strikeout instead of two. The pitches that were hit were a pop fly to Fred and a dribbler to the pitcher's box.

It was weird. The pitch was turning out a lot better than Bernie had expected. When he came off the field he looked up and saw a beaming smile on Dave's face — and of course on Frankie's, too. He was sure that there weren't any guys more proud of him at that moment than those two.

The Rangers garnered four runs during their trip at the plate, then went out on the field, bolstered with the confidence that a seven-run lead can inspire. Bernie wondered how Dave was enjoying it. Of course he had to be. This was what he expected, wasn't it?

Jim Hayes tried to slaughter the first pitch and tripped over his legs.

"Strike one!" boomed the ump.

Jim tried it again. "Strike two!"

And again. "Strike three!"

The ball made its quick rainbow hops around the horn.

"What's he throwing?" Bernie heard Jim say as he returned dejectedly to his bench.

"You just batted against him," replied one of his teammates. "You saw it."

"Yeah, but . . ." That's all Jim had to say.

Mark Pine, the Atoms' center fielder, seemed to have a better idea. He waited out Bernie's pitches, but at the two-two mark he swung and managed to meet the ball. It was a skyrocketing blow. If it had gone as far horizontally as it did vertically, it might have disappeared over the fence. As it was, it dropped down just outside of the third-base foul line and Chuck caught it.

Third baseman Dick Stone waited out Bernie's pitches, too, but with no better luck. He popped up a three-two pitch to Fred to end the bottom of the third inning.

"Okay, Bernie," said Coach Salerno as Bernie came in and lay his glove on top of the dugout. "You can rest for a change. I'll have Jeff finish the game. You did all right, kid. You've really got a mean pitch there."

"Thanks, sir."

"You really changed your delivery from last year, didn't you?" the coach observed, his eyes shaded by the long brim of his cap.

"Right."

The coach peered at him, his thick eyebrows lowering till they came together at the bridge of his nose. "That pitch your own idea, or did somebody tell you about it?"

Bernie looked at him, surprised. "Somebody told me about it."

"What I figured," replied Coach Salerno, grinning. "Your father?"

"No. A friend."

"He must've known Dusty Fowler," said the coach. "Dusty's the only guy I can remember who used to pitch like that. I was just a kid, but I can remember. A lot of guys tried to imitate him, but nobody ever could hold a candle to him. He was the best."

"I read a newspaper clipping about him," said Bernie. "That's what it said."

The coach chuckled. "You keep it up, maybe you'll be the first who can really pitch like him," he said. "But be careful.

Don't twist your wrist too much or it'll get sore and you'll have had it. Throw it without too much effort. You're big and strong, but you're still a kid. Your arms aren't too well developed yet. Know what I mean?"

Bernie nodded. "Yes, I do. I'll be careful."

"Good boy."

The top of the fourth zipped by quickly as Chris had the Rangers ground out to the infield. Then, with catcher Nick Collidino on first base by virtue of a scratch single, Chris came up and scored him at the end of a long triple. The Atoms had their heads out of the water.

Jeff settled down after that and, with some help from his fielders, got the Atoms out. The game went to the sixth inning with both teams scoring two more runs each, ending up with the Rangers winning, 9–3.

It wasn't until Bernie was alone and walking off the field that Frankie and Dave came running up to him, both slapping him enthusiastically on the back.

"You did it, Bernie!" Frankie cried. "You had those Atoms biting the dirt!"

"He did it because he's got it!" said Dave. "And you know what, Bernie? You'll get even better!"

"Don't be so sure," said Bernie pessimistically.

"Why not? There's no other way to go, Bernie, but up."

Down, too, Bernie wanted to say. *For crying out loud, Dave, this was the first time I threw that pitch in a game. It was new to the batters. They could blast me out of the lot the next time!*

The Ranger's first league game was against the Coronas on Thursday, July 6, at four o'clock. Instead of starting on the mound, Bernie found himself on the bench. He couldn't believe it. After his excellent performance the other day, you'd think the coach would pitch him again. Instead, Jeff Eastman was pitching.

The Coronas, batting first, had trouble lining up their swings with Jeff's throws and went down – one, two. The third batter, however, Bobo Johnson, leaned into Jeff's first pitch and poled it for a long home run over the left field fence.

The slam was a shock. An electric jolt. It seemed to sap the strength – the *will* – out of Jeff and the other players. Bernie looked at Coach Salerno and saw the thick eyebrows lower with worry.

Ron Coletti, the Coronas' really big gun, then pounded out a double. His teammates cheered like mad. The Corona fans joined in. The combined sound was a symphony that made it seem as if every person there were for the Coronas.

Then Harry Perkowski walked, Angie Bruno singled, and Tom Bowman doubled, giving the Coronas an indisputable hot lead of four runs. Red Parker ended the merry-go-round by flying out to Ed in right field.

"C'mon! C'mon! C'mon!" yelled the coach, clapping his hands fast as if to pump life back into the guys as they came trotting in like robots. "Get your chins off your chests! Look alive! C'mon! C'mon!"

Maybe the encouragement helped, for Bill Conley, leading off, belted Dick Lunger's first pitch for a double over second base. But that was it. Ed, Deke and Buzz got a piece of the ball, but no hits.

The top of the second inning started off as if it were a new ball game, and Jeff a new pitcher. He faced only three batters, striking out one of them, Jim Black.

As if that scoreless half had had an effect on Dick Lunger, he walked the first man to face him, Tom McDermott. Tom raced to second on Rudy's sacrifice bunt, then scored on Chuck's two-bagger. Fred singled, scoring Chuck, and died there on first as Jeff struck out and Bill grounded out to short.

Bernie saw that the coach's eyebrows had returned to where they belonged and a smile warmed his face; he couldn't help but share the coach's enthusiasm. Now if only Jeff could repeat his pitching prowess of the second inning.

He didn't, though. Both Bobo and Ron singled. Then, after both Harry and Angie went down swinging, Tom smashed a triple to the left field fence and both runners scored.

Bernie saw Jeff's shoulders droop as if a heavy weight had been dropped on him. He looked at the coach. This time not only were the man's eyebrows lowered, but he was muttering to himself, too.

5

"WARM UP, BERNIE," said Coach Salerno quietly.

Putting on his glove, Bernie stepped out of the dugout and went behind the stands with Dick Singer, the utility infielder. He started to throw the submarine pitch, aiming it for the target that Dick held up for him. Sometimes he hit it, sometimes he didn't. He was nervous and hot; he was thinking of that long home run that Bobo had belted off Jeff, the two-baggers off the bats of Ron and Tom, and of Tom's long triple.

Those guys can really hit, he thought. *My submarine pitch could be right up their alley.*

He didn't realize he had two interested spectators until he heard one of them say, "Nothing to worry about, Bernie. Just pitch it to 'em."

He looked at Dave, who had an infectious smile of confidence on his face. Frankie was with him, sharing the same expression.

"I'm nervous," admitted Bernie. "Do I look it?"

"No."

Somebody chuckled from a seat over his head. Bernie glanced up and saw Vincent Steele leering down at him. Next to Vincent was Mick. They looked like a couple of alley cats.

"Now we'll see what that mighty secret

pitch can do," said Vincent. "Right, Bernie?"

His face flaming, Bernie turned away, not answering. From the field he heard loud shouting, and Mick saying, "Hey, man! You guys just scored a run!"

A few minutes later he heard his name called. "Bernie! Let's go!"

"Go chuck 'em, Bernie," teased Vincent. "Give 'em that old secret pitch."

Bernie ignored the banter as he tossed the ball to Dick and started to head for the pitching mound. He was still hot, still nervous.

"Bernie."

He glanced at Dave and saw the serious, proud look on his friend's face.

"Don't pay any attention to Vince and Mick," said Dave. "You can take care of them when the time comes. Just throw that pitch over the plate. Once you let it go, it'll take care of the batter. You'll see."

He's so sure of me, thought Bernie. *So darn sure.*

"You're really something, Dave," he said softly.

"You're my pal, Bernie. You're my best friend. My only real friend. That's why."

"Come on, Bernie!" sounded the coach's voice from the other side of the stands. "Let's get a move on!"

He started to run then and caught the ump's toss as he went by home plate. He got on the mound, threw Fred half a dozen pitches, then watched Dick Lunger step up to the plate to start off the top of the fourth inning.

Dick, one of the tallest guys on the Coronas' team, looked dangerous as he held his bat high off his shoulder and waited for the pitch. Bernie delivered it to him, bringing it up from his knees and releasing it when his hand was directly in front of him. At the last instant he gave the ball a slight twist, barely enough to feel it, for he knew now that too much of a twist might eventually make his wrist sore.

"Ball!"

The Corona fans cheered. "Wow! Look at that pitch!" one of them yelled. "Where did you find that one, Bernie?"

"Ball two!"

The cheer again.

And then, "Strike!"

He wasn't as nervous now.

Dick swung at the next pitch, and also the next – striking out.

Ken Fuller bit the dust, too, striking out on a two-two pitch.

Jim Black stood tall and straight as he watched the pitch come in. He made no

attempt to take the bat off his shoulder until after the second strike pitch. Then he, too, whiffed.

Three strikeouts in a row. The Ranger fans cheered now, letting Bernie know how they felt. He went to the dugout, the guys slapping him on the back, praising him. From the stands directly behind the dugout came the expected cheers of Dave and Frankie. He looked up briefly and saw Dave give him a thumbs-up sign.

"Nice, Bernie!" Dave shouted happily. "Real nice!"

It was the bottom of the fourth now, and Chuck led off. He stood at the plate with his knees bent and his bat held just below his shoulder. Coach Salerno had told him a dozen times to keep his bat up high, but Chuck felt he couldn't hit a barn door that way, so he held the bat the way he felt best. He took two pitches, both strikes, then pounded the third one out to center for an out.

Fred punched a grounder to third for out two; then Bernie came up and took two swings, fouling both. He was nervous again. He was no hitter. He couldn't hit the broad side of a garage with a paddle. But he had fouled two pitches. He was doing *something* right.

He took two balls, then, disappointingly, popped out to short.

The first man Bernie faced in the top of the fifth was Bobo Johnson. Bobo had already uncorked a home run and a single. Bobo was a big kid and had a lot of power. The thought clouded Bernie's mind as he stepped on the rubber, wound up, and delivered. Bobo reared back as the ball swept up toward him. He brought the bat around in a hard, vicious arc, and ended his swing sitting down on the dirt.

"Steerike!" boomed the ump as the ball smacked into Fred's mitt.

The second pitch was a wee bit outside. Bobo took another mighty swing. *Crack!* A blast to deep left! But it was curving . . . curving . . .

"Foul ball!" yelled the base umpire.

Bernie breathed a sigh of relief. That ball had looked like a goner.

Then Bobo popped out to first.

Ron stepped to the plate. He was big, too. Bernie had heard that Ron had already started to shave, but he didn't believe it.

Pow! Ron belted Bernie's first pitch to third. Chuck couldn't get his tail down fast enough and the ball streaked through his legs. The yell from the Corona fans sounded as if Ron had powdered one over the left field fence.

Bernie couldn't get one over the plate against Harry, so he walked him. He walked Angie too and began to wonder if that's what he was going to do the rest of the game – walk the entire Corona team.

Tom Bowman changed the scene for him. Tom swung at two pitches, then boomed one over second that drove in two runs. Red Parker couldn't even get a piece of the ball and struck out. So did Dick. Three outs.

The two runs put the Coronas in front, 8–3. *What is Dave thinking of me and that submarine pitch now?* thought Bernie. *Is that pitch really as good as he had thought it was? Is it as good as I had hoped it would be?*

Dick Singer, batting for Bill, led off in the bottom of the fifth with a walk. Then Arnie Coles, pinch-hitting for Ed, hit a two-two pitch through the shortstop's legs, which helped Arnie a lot, because he had lost his right shoe halfway to first base. Time was called till he got the shoe back on.

Deke poled out a long foul ball, then went down swinging.

Buzz, up next, took a called strike, then suddenly stumbled back and began rubbing his left eye.

"Time!" yelled the ump as he went to see what troubled Buzz. He got out a handkerchief, rubbed at the eye for a few seconds, then put the handkerchief back into his pocket. "Play ball!" he cried.

Buzz stepped back into the box, swung at Dick's next pitch, and *boom!* A blast over the center field fence!

"I'm glad he got that thing out of his eye, whatever it was," said the coach, grinning, as Buzz trotted around the bases. It was 8–6 now, the Coronas still in front.

Neither Tom nor Rudy got on to Dick's pitches, and the game went into the sixth inning. Bernie's submarine pitch seemed to work like a miracle this time as he struck out the three batters who faced him.

"Okay, men!" cried Coach Salerno, standing up in front of the dugout and clapping his hands to psyche up the guys. "This is our last chance! We need three runs! All we have to do to get 'em is hit, right? All right – let's hit!"

Chuck, leading off, flied out to left field.

"I said *hit,* Chuck!" yelled the coach. "Okay, Fred. Bust one."

Fred did, driving a sizzling grounder just inside the first base bag for a double.

Then Bernie stepped to the plate, wishing that somebody would pinch-hit for him. He stood and waited for Dick to pour in his first pitch.

6

DICK GOT ON THE RUBBER, looked over at Fred, then poured it in. Bernie, his heart almost still, kept his eyes on the ball as it came in, straight as a string. It was heading down the pipe.

He swung. *Crack!* He felt a faint electric shock as the bat connected. He saw the ball streak over second for a hit. Dropping his bat, he bolted for first. The crowd roared as Fred crossed the plate.

Bernie stood on the bag with both feet. He felt proud, happy. *It's my lucky day,* he thought. *It has to be. I'm usually a lousy hitter.*

The Ranger fans groaned as Dick grounded out. One more out and the game would go to the Coronas.

Then Arnie walked, advancing Bernie to second.

"Drive it, Deke!" yelled Arnie.

Deke drove it, a piping hot double over third base. Bernie ran to third and then home as if his shirttail were on fire. Arnie came in behind him, sliding safely over the plate a fraction of a second ahead of the shortstop's throw.

It was over. The Rangers had copped their first league game, 9–8.

Dave and Frankie came down from the stands and slapped Bernie on the back as if he were the hero.

"Nice game, Bernie," Dave exclaimed, beaming with pride. "You played a heck of a game. You know that?"

"I was just lucky," replied Bernie.

Vincent Steel and Mick Devlan came forward, both wearing devil-may-care smiles.

"Well, I guess you *can* be hit, Bernie," said Vincent.

"Who said I couldn't be?"

"Your buddy here. Dave. And your little brother, Frankie."

Bernie looked at them. *Can't you guys keep your traps shut?* his look said.

"Those hits weren't solid," said Dave defensively. "Another fraction of an inch one way or another and they would've been strikeouts."

Vince pretended to ignore him. He said to Bernie, "We're playing you guys next Tuesday. Mick and I made a bet that one of us will knock your submarine pitch back into the sea." They started away, grinning. "Adios, amigos!"

"Punks," grumbled Frankie.

Bernie looked at his brother and Dave. "Okay. Which of you guys told them?"

"Told them what?" asked Dave curiously.

"That it's called a submarine pitch."

There was silence for a moment. Then Frankie confessed. "I did. Nothing wrong about that, is there? Its name is no secret, anyway, is it?"

"Nothing is secret about it now," said Dave. "Now that they've seen you pitch. Don't be sore at him, Bernie."

"I'm not," replied Bernie, trying to hide his chagrin. "Come on. Let's go home."

When Bernie arrived home his mother said that she had good news for him. But first, who won the game? He told her,

Frankie adding the frills, telling her about Bernie's great pitching, about his getting a hit, then tying up the score.

"Hey!" she cried, her face lighting up like a sunflower. "You going to be another Carl Stramski?"

"Yastrzemski, Mom," corrected Ann-Marie. "We've told you that a dozen times before. Anyhow, he wasn't a pitcher. He was a fielder."

"What's the good news you've got for me?" asked Bernie.

"You've got a job," she said. "Mrs. Benson would like you to paint her fence."

His eyes lit up. "When?"

"As soon as you can. I told her you could do it tomorrow. Okay?"

Excitement bubbled inside him as he thought about it a minute. "Right! I'll do it in the morning. Oh, boy! Ten bucks an hour okay, Mom?"

"Ten bucks? Who do you think you are, anyway? A big-time contractor? Make it five. That's enough. When you become an expert and gain a good reputation, *then* you can charge ten bucks."

He shrugged resignedly. "Do I have to buy the paint, too?"

"No. She's got the paint. How much money have you earned toward your bike so far?"

"Onc hundred forty-four dollars," he said. "I need almost three times that much."

"Maybe you'll have to advertise for jobs," she said, smiling.

The next day, bright and early, he went over to Mrs. Benson's, got the paint, and started on the fence. It was a brand-new one, about five feet high, and enclosed her entire yard. Mrs. Benson was a widow and lived alone, except for two canaries, a parrot, and three cats who kept her company.

It was close to eleven o'clock, and Bernie had two-thirds of the fence painted, when someone came up the side-walk behind him and yelled, "Hi!"

He whirled, startled out of his wits. As he did he felt his foot bang against the paint can and heard the instant, heart-sickening sound of spilling paint. Quickly he grabbed the can and righted it, but what was left was barely enough to fill a cup. The rest of it, about half a gallon, had turned a small patch of lawn from bright green to creamy white.

"Wow!" cried Vincent Steele. "I'm sorry, Bernie! I didn't mean to scare you like that!"

Bernie turned and glared at him. Vince was on his bike. With him was Mick on his.

PAINT

"Maybe you didn't, but you did," said Bernie angrily. "Now I'll have to buy what I need out of the money I'm earning."

The paint had cost Mrs. Benson $19.98. He had seen the price on the lid.

"Let's shove off, Vince," said Mick. "Anyway, it's not all your fault. He kicked it over."

"I'm really sorry, Bernie," said Vince, as he started to pedal away.

"Sure," mumbled Bernie.

His heart aching, he finished painting with what was left of the paint, then stood a long minute thinking before he went to the door of the house and knocked. The ache changed to fear. What was Mrs. Benson going to say when he told her what happened? Would she get mad and fire him right off the bat?

He heard her footsteps. Then the door

opened and there she stood, tall and gray-haired, a rather plain-looking woman who didn't look as if she smiled a lot.

"Hello, Bernie," she greeted him. "Are you done already?"

"No, Mrs. Benson. I—I'm out of paint." His tongue felt dry as paper. "I spilled about half a can of it."

"You did?" She stared at him as if it weren't possible, then let a smile warm her face. "Well, accidents will happen," she said. "Come in a minute and I'll figure out what we'll do."

He went in and sat down at the kitchen table, noticing an aroma that could come from only one delicious delicacy—doughnuts. His mouth watered.

"How much more have you got to do?" she asked, grabbing a napkin from a pack on the counter. She went to the stove on which stood a large aluminum pot, picked out a powdered-sugar doughnut, and brought it to him.

"Not much," he answered. "Maybe twenty feet."

"Good. Suppose you leave the rest for tomorrow. I'll go into town in the morning and buy two quarts of paint. That should do it, don't you think?"

She talked to him about it as though he were an expert on paints.

"I think so," he answered, accepting the big, soft, fragrant doughnut. He suddenly realized that he wasn't frightened anymore. She wasn't mad at him; she wasn't going to fire him. "Thanks, Mrs. Benson," he said.

He looked at the crimson spot on the doughnut where she had inserted the jelly.

"What's the matter, Bernie?" Mrs. Benson asked curiously. "What are you thinking?"

It's $19.98 a gallon, he was thinking. *Two quarts would come to at least ten or eleven dollars.*

"You can take the money out of my pay, Mrs. Benson," he told her.

7

MRS. BENSON PHONED him the next morning. She had bought the paint, she said, and he could come over and finish the job anytime that it was convenient for him.

Bernie remembered that the Rangers were playing the Sharks at four o'clock. If he got started right away—it wasn't quite eleven—he should have the job completed before one, giving him time enough to rest before the game.

"Okay, Mrs. Benson," he said. "I'll come right over."

He finished the job, using all of one can and a small portion of the other. Mentally he figured that he had worked four hours altogether. At five dollars an hour that added up to twenty dollars. Subtract ten dollars from that, plus tax, for the extra paint Mrs. Benson had to buy, and that would leave him about ten dollars. Ten lousy dollars, just because that crumb, Vince, had caused him to spill half a can of paint.

Mrs. Benson came out and looked at his job. She didn't like the sight of the spilled paint and asked Bernie to dig it up with a shovel. Other than that she said his paint job was fine. She didn't say "excellent," she just said "fine." Which wasn't as good, and which could mean that she probably wished she didn't have to give him the ten lousy dollars.

He got the shovel and dug up the paint,

smoothing up the dirt afterward till it was impossible to tell that paint had been spilled there. Then he went to the house to tell Mrs. Benson he was finished.

She smiled at him and handed him an envelope. "Thanks, Bernie," she said. "Whenever I have any other work around the house I can't do myself, I'll call on you."

"Thanks, Mrs. Benson," he answered. "I'm sorry about spilling the paint."

"Oh, forget it," she said. "It could happen to anybody."

He started away, somehow feeling that no matter how much work Mrs. Benson might have in the future, she would never call on him again.

He had almost reached the sidewalk when he heard the door open and Mrs. Benson's voice. "Bernie! Just a minute! I almost forgot something!"

She was holding a napkin with a doughnut in it. "Here," she said, smiling brightly. "I made a couple of dozen to take to our women's club last night, but I made sure to save another one for you. You do like them, don't you?"

Bernie's face brightened up like a lamp. "I sure do, Mrs. Benson!" he exclaimed as he accepted it from her. "Thanks, Mrs. Benson."

He ate it on his way home; it tasted just as good as the one he had yesterday. Mrs. Benson was a peach, he decided.

He got home, took the envelope to his room, and went to the bathroom to wash up.

"Well," said AnnMarie, finishing a sandwich at the kitchen table, "did you earn so much you're going to keep it a secret?"

"After all the deductions," said Frankie,

leaning against the doorjamb, "he figures he'll get about ten bucks."

"Well, there's no sense crying over spilled paint," said Mrs. Shantz. "And don't tease your brother. It wasn't all his fault the paint spilled."

When Bernie was finished he went and sat at the kitchen table while his mother warmed up some soup and fixed him a sandwich. He was tired. It was a good thing that the game was at four; he had plenty of time to rest.

"Well, why the big secret?" AnnMarie asked again. "Aren't you going to tell us how much you earned?"

"I know how much I *earned*," he said sullenly. "I just don't care to see how much I *got*."

Nevertheless he went to his room, picked up the envelope, and tore it open. There were two bills in it; he could barely see the figure 5 in a corner where one bill was curled slightly. *Two fives*, he figured.

Then he took out the other bill—and his eyes widened. A twenty! Mrs. Benson had given him twenty-five dollars!

He rushed into the other room, waving it over his head like a flag. "Look what she paid me!" he cried. "Twenty-five dollars! Can you believe it? Twenty-five dollars! Oh, I love you, Mrs. Benson! I love you with my whole heart!"

His mom, AnnMarie, and Frankie smiled happily at him.

Dave called at two o'clock. He said that his mother was going to drive him to the game shortly after three and would Bernie and Frankie like to ride with him?

"Sure," said Bernie.

After Bernie hung up he realized that it was strange that Dave's mother should be driving him to the game. Dave had always walked before. *Never* ridden.

"Something must really be wrong with Dave Grant, Ma," he said. "His mother's driving him to the game, stopping here for Frankie and me first. Mrs. Grant ever tell you about him?"

"No. And maybe you're drawing some wrong conclusions," said Mrs. Shantz. "Maybe Mrs. Grant has to make a trip that way and is killing two birds with one stone."

"Could be," said Bernie. "Just the same, Dave has been acting funny lately, Ma. He seems to want to do a lot of things, then gets pooped in no time at all. I don't think he's well."

"I wouldn't worry about it," said Mrs. Shantz. "I'm sure that his parents know if he's troubled by some illness. Why don't *you* get a good rest before they show up?

You need it after working so hard this morning."

He lay down in his room and slept for almost an hour. At ten after three Mrs. Grant drove up with Dave, picked up Bernie and Frankie, drove them to the ball park, and left.

Bernie wanted to ask Dave if his mother had an errand to do or if she were driving directly home. Then he changed his mind. It wasn't his business, he told himself. And if Dave were sick or something, and didn't want to tell anyone about it, that was *his* business.

Just the same, Dave was his good friend and it was hard to ignore the way he'd been behaving lately.

Both teams took their batting and infield practices. Then, promptly at four, the game started. The Rangers were at bat first, with Bernie in the lineup. On the mound for the Sharks was Luke Kish, a tall right-hander with a mop of curly black hair that his baseball cap was barely large enough to sit on.

Bill took a called strike, then asked for time out and ran to the dugout for another bat. When he was settled in the batter's box again he leaned into a high pitch and blazed it to Vince in left field for the first out. Ed connected with a double and Deke walked, bringing a rousing cheer from the Ranger fans and Buzz up to the plate.

Luke brushed two strikes past him, missed the corner on the next three pitches, then fired one on a level with Buzz's knees. *Crack!* Buzz sent it spark-flying to second base. The result was a quick double play, second to first.

Disappointed that they couldn't score

even one of the two runners, the Rangers gathered up their gloves and ambled out to their positions. Bernie tossed in three warm-up pitches, then stood on the rubber and faced his first man, Tim MacDonald. Tim was the shortest kid on the Sharks. He must have been ordered to just stand there and not swing, because that's just what he did, and it earned him a free pass to first.

Jess Miller tried to bunt the first pitch, missed, then tried to bunt the second pitch and missed that one, too. Then he struck out.

The ball sailed around the horn.

Bernie measured Butch Ecker's height with a calm glance, then fired two inside pitches past him. Two corner cutters evened up the count, two and two. On deck was Vince, swinging two bats with metal doughnuts on them.

Bernie felt his heart pound as he got ready to throw the next pitch. Vince really looked sure of himself. What had he said? *Mick and I made a bet that one of us will knock your submarine pitch back into the sea.*

That guy really bugs me, thought Bernie.

He stretched, then blazed in the ball, bringing it up from his knees, and giving it a slight twist just as he released it. *Crack!* The ball looped over short for a Texas leaguer hit!

Up to the plate strode Vince, a confident smile on his lips. It lingered there as he waited for Bernie's first pitch.

CRACK!

The blow was loud and solid as the ball shot out to deep left, curving toward the foul line. A yell broke simultaneously from the fans, then deflated to a sad groan as the ball struck foul by inches.

"You was robbed, Vince!" yelled a Shark fan.

"He was lucky, Bernie!" came another voice, one that Bernie recognized. "He hit it by accident!"

He glanced in the direction from which the sound had come and saw both Dave and Frankie sitting halfway up the stands behind the backstop. Dave waved to him, while Frankie sat quiet and composed beside him, indifferent to the long foul shot.

Bernie breezed in two more pitches that Vince let go by. Two balls, one strike. Then Vince swung, this time getting just a piece of the ball. Bernie pitched again. Outside. Three and two.

He stepped off the mound, rubbed the ball nervously, then got back on again. He stretched, delivered, and watched the ball shoot up toward the plate, coming close to Vince. Too close. Vince pulled his bat back ready to swing, then tried to dodge the ball as it headed directly at him. He wasn't quick enough and the ball struck him a glancing blow on the hip.

A gasp tore from Bernie as he stared at

Vince, wondering if he were hurt. But apparently Vince wasn't, for he dropped his bat and calmly started for first, loading the bases.

"Afraid I'd sink one of your submarine pitches, Bernie?" he said.

Bernie didn't answer. Hitting Vince bothered him, though. The last thing he wanted to do was hit a batter.

Then he walked in a run by giving Bob Kolowski a free pass.

Fred Button called time and trotted out to the mound. "You okay, Bernie?" he asked.

"I'm okay," said Bernie. Sweat glistened on his face. The sun was hot, but it wasn't the sun's heat that bothered him. It was hitting Vince.

"Relax," said Fred. "Just get those pitches over, that's all."

"Right."

He did, and struck out the next two men.

Rangers 0, Sharks 1.

Tom McDermott led off the top of the second with a streaking single through short. Rudy Sims bunted him to second, but that was as far as he got as Chuck and Fred flied and grounded out, respectively.

Mick Devlan, leading off for the Sharks, walked. Luke Kish got a feel of Bernie's submarine pitch with a foul tick, then grounded out. Tim, batting for the second time, popped out to short, and Jess landed on his bottom as he went down swinging.

Bernie's heart pounded as he stepped up to the plate to lead off the top of the third inning. He couldn't explain it, but he always hated being the leadoff batter in any inning.

He took two called strikes, then held

his breath as Luke breezed two inside pitches by him. Both were teasers for him to bite on.

Then Luke fired in a fast ball that came up along Bernie's chest. Bernie cut at it, swinging harder than he had so far this year, and met the ball squarely. It sailed out to deep left like a white rocket, but it was a mile high and gave Vince plenty of time to get under it. Vince put it away easily and Bernie, already halfway to first, slowed down, turned, and ran back to the bench. *Should've known I'd never smash one over the fence,* he thought dispiritedly.

The top of the batting order was up again. Bill stepped to the plate, then called time to tie his shoelaces. Then he knocked the dirt off the soles of his shoes with his bat before stepping into the batting box.

"You sure you're ready now?" the umpire asked him.

Bill nodded, smiling.

Luke pitched. *Crack!* Bill drilled it over short for a single.

Ed struck out. Then Deke, after fouling two pitches to the backstop screen, spiked a down-the-middle pitch close to the left field foul line for a triple, scoring Bill. Buzz ripped a single through short, scoring Deke, then Tom flied out, ending the two-run rally.

Butch was the first man up for the Sharks in the bottom of the third. As he rubbed the toes of his shoes into the dirt to dig in for Bernie's pitch, Bernie took the time to look behind the backstop screen. He saw Frankie, but not Dave. A sudden chill rippled through him. What had happened to him? Why wasn't he there? He had an intuition that something awful had happened to his friend.

He turned his attention back to the game and saw that Butch was ready. He stretched, delivered.

"Ball!" boomed the ump.

Bernie drilled in another. "Ball two!"

He caught Fred's toss back and glanced up at the stands. Dave was still missing.

He fired in a strike, then two more balls.

"Take your base!" yelled the ump.

Bernic did no better with Vince, nor with Bob. Three walks in a row and not an out.

Fred called time out again and ran out to ask Bernie if he were all right.

"Sure, I'm all right," Bernie answered stiffly.

"You sure aren't throwing as if you are," Fred answered.

"Well, I am. Get back where you belong, will you?"

Fred stared at him, then spun on his heels and trotted back to his position.

Sam was up. He had struck out the first time at bat. He didn't look dangerous, but in *this* inning nobody had to get a free pass to first base. It seemed all you needed was a uniform and a bat on your shoulder.

Oh, man, what am I thinking! Bernie asked himself. *All I'm doing is walking the guys. Why doesn't the coach take me out? Can't he see that I'm missing the plate by a yard?*

He stepped on the rubber, eyed the plate, and tried to concentrate on the pitch. He couldn't. He could only think about Dave. Something had happened to him. He was sure of it. Right after the half-inning was over he'd ask Frankie.

He wouldn't be able to continue playing without knowing.

He stretched, and delivered a sidearm pitch that was down the pipe. Sam met it with the fat part of his bat and Bernie heard the message: *It's gone!* The blow to left center was a three-bagger for Sam and the end of the line for Bernie.

Coach Salerno took him out and put in Jeff Eastman.

"You feel all right, Bernie?" the coach asked as he met Bernie in front of the dugout.

"Yeah. I'm okay. I just can't get it over, that's all."

"You look as if you've got your mind in Timbuktu. Sit it out. Maybe you'll come back to earth after a while."

Then the coach squeezed his shoulder lightly and laughed. "I'm kidding, Bernie.

You're just having one of those days. It'll pass."

Bernie shrugged, started for the dugout, and looked up at the stands again. A peculiar sensation stirred through him and he began to feel foolish.

Dave was there now, and he looked perfectly fine.

9

ANDY FLIED OUT to left. Mick popped out to Bill and Luke grounded out, ending the Shark's fat half-inning. Rangers 2, Sharks 4.

Maybe Jeff should've started instead of me, Bernie thought.

Rudy Sims led off in the top of the fourth with a series of foul balls, then struck out. Chuck doubled. Fred, belting three fouls in a row, finally popped out to Mick.

Bernie had visions of the game going down the drain and of Vince popping off to him, uttering sarcastic remarks. He had a good idea why Vince acted that way toward him; it had started shortly after track season, when Bernie had outrun Vince in the 50- and 100-yard dashes. That had qualified Bernie to run against other schools in the league and had earned him over half a dozen first prizes. Vince hated to see that somebody was better than he was.

Jeff waited out Luke's pitches to the limit, then cracked the three-two pitch to short. Tim MacDonald muffed it and Jeff was safe on first. Then Bill lined out a streaking single, scoring Chuck. Ed flied out, and that was it.

Tim, leading off for the Sharks, lined Jeff's first pitch to center field for a hit, scooted to second on Jess's sacrifice bunt, then scored on Butch's shot to left field. Vince popped a foul fly to Deke, who caught the ball near the Sharks' dugout. Then Bob bashed a double over third base to score Butch, and Sam Norton grounded out, ending the Sharks two-run rally.

Buzz's triple, and Rudy's single, gave a breath of life to the Rangers as they picked up one run in the top of the fifth. The Sharks couldn't score at their turn at bat, but held the Rangers scoreless too in the top of the sixth, and won 6–4.

Bernie hoped to avoid meeting Vince as he left the field, but Vince cornered him almost immediately.

"What happened to your submarine pitch, Bernie?" he asked. "Run out of fuel? It didn't even surface!"

"Why don't you go and haunt somebody else for a while, Vince?" Frankie snapped.

Vince punched him lightly on the shoulder, hardly enough to hurt. "What are you — your brother's dummy?" He laughed then and dropped back, waiting for Mick to join him.

"Why's he like that?" Dave asked as he, Bernie, and Frankie started off the field. "He picks on you as if he's sore at you about something."

"He is sore, because I beat him out in track," said Bernie. "I've got ribbons to show for it and he doesn't."

"So *that's* what bugs him." Dave shook his head. "I don't know about him. He's a good baseball player. Real good. What else does he want?"

"He wants to show me that he can hit my submarine pitch," replied Bernie.

"He won't, though. Not if you're on. What happened to you today, anyway? Frankie told me that you hit Vince, then couldn't get a pitch over the plate."

Bernie looked at him. "That's right. But

what happened to *you?* Where did you disappear to?"

Dave shrugged. "I got thirsty and went for a drink."

Bernie stared at him. "That's all you did? You sure?"

Dave matched his stare. "That's all I did. I'm sure. Why? Was that what bothered you? My not being there for a little while?"

Bernie nodded, letting out a deep breath.

"Let's forget it, shall we?" he said, but he wondered if Dave was telling the whole truth.

The Rangers' next scheduled game was against the Atoms. Jeff wasn't present and Bernie figured he'd have to pitch the whole game. Well, if he was going good, he wouldn't mind it. Anyway, he shouldn't have to worry much. They had beat the pants off the Atoms in the practice game, 9–3.

The Rangers batted first. Pitching for the Atoms was a short, stout kid called Petey Waterman. Bill, leading off, looked over Petey's first two pitches, both strikes, then laced the next one into right center for a long triple. Ed flied out, but both Deke and Buzz pounded the ball for safe hits. Then Tom grounded out.

Rudy found the handle of Petey's pitches again and walloped out a double, scoring Deke and advancing Buzz to third. Bernie felt relieved now that he could get out there with at least two runs to back him up. "Come on, Chuck!" he yelled. "Bring 'im in!"

But Buzz died on third as Chuck flied out to center fielder Mark Pine.

The first batter to face Bernie was the

skinny kid, Ralph Benz, who looked like the letter Z as he stood bent over the plate. Bernie wound up and threw his submarine pitch — even the *Lake Center News* was calling it that — and got Ralph swinging at the air. Ralph went down after four pitches.

Jim Hayes popped up to Chuck. But Hank Dooley was stubborn. He kept ticking Bernie's pitches as if he were seeking a record for fouls. Finally, after the sixth tick, he flied out to Bill.

In the top of the second, Fred got on to Petey's second pitch, belting it for a double between center and left fields. Bernie, getting the coach's signal to bunt, couldn't latch on to a satisfying pitch, and finally walked. Bill popped out. Then Ed came through with a high, rainbow drive over Mark Pine's head in center field that hit the fence and ricocheted back. It was good for a triple and scored Fred and Bernie. Deke tried to kill Petey's pitches —falling down twice on his rear—then popped up to the catcher, Nick Collodino. Buzz grounded out to short to end the hot inning.

Bernie felt as pleased as he ever had when he picked up his glove and walked out to the mound. The day was like a hot oven, but he didn't mind. His submarine pitch was working.

He glanced up at the stands and saw Dave sitting with Frankie, Mom and Dad. Dad had the day off, and Bernie was glad to see him there. Dad hadn't seen a game this year yet, so he hadn't seen Bernie's new submarine pitch.

Bernie looked at the batter, Mark Pine. Mark was a big, powerful kid. He had the eyes of a hawk. Bernie wound up, delivered. The ball came up from his knees and shot toward the plate. Mark reared back and swung. *Swoosh!* He missed the pitch by six inches. Two more swings and he was out.

The Ranger fans roared.

Dick Stone missed with two swings, then popped out to short. Foxy Mattoon waited them out, then laced the three-two pitch to Bill, who piped it over to first for the third out.

4–0, Rangers.

In the top of the third Tom, leading off, lambasted a triple against the right field fence, then perished on the sack as Petey shot down the next three guys on strike-outs.

Needle Hall, who was even skinnier than Ralph Benz, led off for the Atoms. He pulled a surprise, bunting Bernie's first pitch down toward third for a base hit. Nick Collodino followed suit with another surprise bunt; then Petey looped a single over short, driving in the Atoms' first run.

Now the Atom fans let everybody know they were there, too.

The rally continued, Ralph and Jim both knocking out singles.

"There goes your submarine pitch, Bernie!" yelled Needle, who was now coaching at third.

Hank Dooley ticked the ball twice this time, then popped out to short. Mark, up next, tried again to smash the ball out of the county and again went down swinging. Dick Stone pounded out a double, scoring two runs, then Foxy struck out. Rangers 4, Atoms 5.

Bernie felt a big lump in his stomach as he walked off the mound. Darn it! The pitch just wasn't working again. It was too *erratic*. Was that the word?

"How's it coming in, Fred?" he asked

the catcher as they sat down together in the dugout.

"It's too low, I think," said Fred. "It's not coming up."

"Bernie, you're up," said the coach. "Get on, okay?"

Bernie did, driving a long shot over Hank Dooley's head that only missed going over the fence by inches. He stopped on third for his longest hit of the season.

The game was delayed a minute as the coach worked an eyelash out of Bill Conley's left eye. Then the shortstop walked to the plate and drilled a single through short, scoring Bernie. Ed got a free pass to first, advancing Bill to second. Petey got Deke out on a change-up, then tried to pull the same trick on Buzz. But Buzz connected the ball solidly, driving it like a meteor over the left field fence for a long home run. Tom and Rudy both got out, but four runs had scored. 8–5, Rangers.

The Atoms failed to get a man on during their turn at bat, and held the Rangers to one run in the top of the fifth.

They scored once when they came to bat, then kept the Rangers scoreless in the top of the last inning. With two outs in the bottom of the sixth, they got things rolling again. Foxy started it by winning a free ticket to first. Then Needle socked a crazy dribbler down to short, which Bill muffed.

Nervous now, and fearing that a hit might start a real hitting spree, Bernie threw four pitches to Nick Collodino, all balls.

The bases were loaded, and Petey was up.

10

PETEY WAS A fair batter. He already had a single to his credit. A long hit could clear the bases and give the Rangers something to worry about.

"Ball!" yelled the ump as Bernie blazed in his first pitch.

What am I going to do—walk him, too? Bernie asked himself.

He concentrated on pitching then, and placed the next one over the plate. He grooved the next one in the same place, and Petey swung wildly.

"Strike two!" yelled the ump.

The next pitch snaked up and Petey did it again.

"Strike three!" boomed the ump.

The game was over. Bernie sighed with relief.

He ran off the mound, the Ranger fans applauding him. His parents and Ann-Marie came down from the stands and praised him, too.

"I like that pitch of yours," his father said, his eyes dancing. "So that's your famous submarine pitch, is it?"

Bernie beamed. "That's what they call it," he said. "You know that Dave Grant told me about it and showed me how to throw it, don't you?"

"Yes, I heard that," said his father. "I guess you owe Dave quite a lot."

Bernie nodded. "Yes, I do, Dad."

He looked for Dave and Frankie and saw them coming. They showered Bernie with some of their own brand of praise, then they all walked home together. Bernie couldn't help noticing how pale Dave looked.

"You okay, Dave?" he asked. "You look pale."

Dave shrugged. "I'm okay," he said.

You're lying, thought Bernie. *You're sick. You must be sick if your face is almost the color of milk.*

At Bernie's house Dave asked if he could telephone his mother.

"You are sick, aren't you?" said Bernie.

"Well, just tired. I thought I'd ask my mom to come for me."

"Why should you do that?" said Mr. Shantz. "I'll drive you home."

"But—"

"No buts," said Mr. Shantz, and went to the garage to get his car. "Come on."

Bernie watched Dave get into the car

and ride off. Something was definitely wrong with Dave, he was sure of it. But what? That's what he wanted to know.

A few days later, shortly after lunch, Bernie got a phone call from Dave. It was July 18, the day the Rangers were to meet the Sharks for the second time.

"Hi, Dave," said Bernie. "What's up?"

"I was wondering if you'd like to walk uptown with me," said Dave.

"Why?"

"I'll tell you when I see you."

"Okay. See you in a little while."

Bernie told his mother where he was going, then walked over to Dave's house. Dave met him outside and they started to walk uptown.

"I've been saving up dough for a model," said Dave, a tone of pride in his voice. "The *Constitution.*"

"Hey, that's great."

"I didn't want to mention it on the phone because I don't want my parents to know about it," explained Dave. "Not yet, anyway."

Bernie stared at him. "You getting it for them?"

"No. It's for me. But I want to surprise them just the same."

In about fifteen minutes they reached the business district. They came to a hobby shop and Dave paused in front of its large display window. It was jam-packed with art crafts and models of airplanes, cars, railroads, and ships.

"Oh, no!" Dave cried.

"What's the matter?" said Bernie.

"It's gone! The *Constitution*'s gone!" Dave almost sobbed.

He rushed into the building, Bernie at his heels. *It must be some model,*

HOBBY SHOP
U.S.S. CONSTITUTION

he thought, *if that's the way Dave feels about it.*

Inside the store Dave paused. Together the boys searched the dozens of craft-loaded shelves for the model of the *Constitution.*

Suddenly Dave shouted, pointing, "There it is, Bernie! Thank goodness it wasn't sold!"

He raced around a counter loaded with figurines and stopped in front of a row of shelves on which ship models were displayed. There, at eye level, was one of the most beautiful ship models Bernie had ever seen.

"That's it," said Dave. "Isn't it a beauty, Bern?"

"It sure is," admitted Bernie.

A tall, dark-haired man came forward. His eyes smiled behind his rimless glasses. "Can I help you?" he asked.

"That model," said Dave, pointing at the *Constitution*. "How much is it?"

The clerk smiled and rubbed his nose. "Forty-nine ninety-five."

Bernie stared at Dave and saw that he looked stricken.

"It's a gorgeous model," said the clerk. "One of the finest in our store."

"I know," Dave said. "I'm sure it's worth every penny. Thanks."

They walked out of the store, Dave's hands deep inside his pockets.

"You don't have enough money to buy it. Right?" said Bernie.

"Right. All I've got is thirty dollars. I never dreamed it would cost that much. Forty-nine ninety-five. Wow."

Several people were assembled in front of Woolworth's, watching a guy demonstrating a yo-yo. The boys stopped to watch, too.

Bernie thought about the money he was saving toward a brand-new bike. If it weren't for the bike . . .

"I can loan you the rest," he said abruptly. "I'm saving for a bike, but by the time I get the balance that I need, you might be able to pay me back."

"No, thanks," said Dave. "I'll get it myself. Somehow, I'll get it."

"But, why not? It's not like I'm giving it to you. You're going to pay me back."

Dave shook his head. "No. And that's final, Bern."

They walked a while in silence. Then Bernie, to break the mood, asked, "How did you raise your money for the model, Dave?"

"Baby-sitting. How do you raise yours?"

"Different ways. Painting a fence was my last job."

Suddenly he glanced at a clock on the

wall of a store. "Hey!" he cried. "It's three-thirty! I'll be late for the game!"

His heart pounded and sweat began to ooze from his forehead. What burned Coach Salerno more than anything was one of his players showing up late at a game.

They started to run. Bernie, a fast runner and with considerable endurance, didn't realize how far Dave trailed behind him until he had covered about five blocks. When he looked back Dave was almost two blocks behind him! And Dave was *walking!*

"Dave!" Bernie shouted. "You okay?"

Dave waved him on. "Go ahead! Don't wait for me!"

Bernie frowned. *What shall I do?* he wondered. *Suppose Dave gets sick and nobody's near him? I can't go on without him.*

He waited. Dave was literally dragging his feet.

"You okay?" Bernie asked as Dave finally reached him.

"Just tired," confessed Dave. "I told you to go on. I'll feel terrible if you're going to be late because of me, Bern. And you will be late. Go ahead. Please!"

"Are you sure you'll be all right?" Bernie asked.

"I'm sure."

"Okay. See you at the game."

11

BERNIE RACED ALL the way home, wriggled into his uniform, and then ran all the way to the ball park, arriving there just as the game was about to begin. Dick Singer, the utility infielder, was ready to go out on the mound.

"Nice time to get around!" the coach snapped at Bernie. "Where've you been?"

"Uptown," Bernie panted.

"You must've run all the way. What kind of a game do you expect to pitch all pooped out like that?"

"Where's Jeff?" Bernie asked, looking around for the alternate pitcher.

"He's home nursing a cold. Nice, huh? Well, don't just stand there. Get out there on the mound and throw some warm-ups. Dick, relax before you get all pooped out yourself."

Dick Singer took a deep breath and blew it out, apparently not pleased that he wasn't starting. He tossed his glove on top of the dugout, then clambered down into the dugout and sat down.

Bernie walked out to the mound – still tired from the long run – threw in a few warm-up pitches, then stepped to one side as Fred beelined a throw to Tom at second base. Tom tossed it to Chuck who relayed it back to Bernie.

Well, what kind of a game is this going to be? Bernie asked himself. He had already gotten a strike on himself by running all that distance from uptown. After that no kid in his right mind could expect to make a decent showing pitching to a good team like the Sharks, let alone win the game.

On top of that worry there was another. Dave. Bernie started to sweat just thinking about his friend. Darn it all, he should have ignored Dave's plea to go to the game and stayed with him. Dave could have gotten awfully ill and collapsed on the way home.

I shouldn't have run, he told himself despairingly. *Then Dave would not have run, and we both would have arrived at the game in good shape. So what if I were late? Better late than taking a chance of Dave's collapsing from whatever he's suffering from.*

In spite of his misery he laid his first

two pitches right on target to Tim MacDonald, the Sharks' leadoff hitter. His next pitch was outside. Then Tim tied onto the next one for a clean single; Bernie watched helplessly as the ball streaked through the infield.

Jess bunted Tim to second and reached first base safely as Chuck Haley, fielding the bunt, threw wide. Both runners advanced a base, and Butch Ecker came up.

Butch leaned into Bernie's first pitch, connecting solidly for a double between left and center that scored the two runners.

Bernie's spirit sank like a lead weight. Two runs already, and not yet an out.

Then Vince stepped to the plate, digging his toes into the dirt as he got ready for Bernie's first pitch. He wasn't smiling now; he was serious, as if nothing were more important to him at this moment than blasting Bernie's pitch out of the lot.

Bernie glanced briefly at the stands. Had Dave arrived yet, or had he gone home? Was he okay? *What kind of a friend am I, anyway,* thought Bernie, *for leaving him there on the street? Oh, man. Just for a lousy baseball game.*

He stepped on the mound, stretched, and delivered. The moment he released the ball he knew that the pitch still lacked the speed and zip to make it effective.

Crack! Vince's solid smash proved it. The ball sizzled out to right center for a two-bagger, bringing in another run for the Sharks. Vince stood on the sack, smiling triumphantly and clapping.

Bob Kolowski then popped out and Sam Norton flied out. But Andy Cornwall connected safely, driving a shot past Buzz for a hit.

"Your submarine pitch is sunk, Bernie!"

Vince yelled to him as he rounded third base toward home. "You might as well get ready for the showers!"

Bernie tried to ignore him as he caught the throw in, rubbed the ball, and hoped – hoped for the tiredness to creep out of his body, the ache to leave his muscles. Mick Devlan was up next, and Bernie got back on the mound, intent on making Mick end the rally.

He didn't. Mick belted the first pitch over second for a single, advancing Andy to third.

A lump lodged in Bernie's throat. He was pitching the worst he had ever pitched. Why didn't the coach pull him?

But Coach Salerno was sitting there in the dugout as if he didn't have a worry in the world.

Luke Kish, the Sharks' pitcher, ended the fat inning with a one-bouncer directly back to Bernie, who threw to first for the third out.

Four big runs. It looked like the start of a slaughter.

Bernie went in sulking and sat down at the end of the bench. He was certainly glad he wasn't one of the first batters. He needed the rest; he had been standing out there long enough.

He was surprised when the coach came and sat down beside him.

"You're probably wondering why I didn't take you out," said the coach. Bernie shrugged. "Well, let me tell you. You're a little tired from having run from uptown, which was a stupid thing to do in the first place. Right? But, by the second inning – or maybe the third – you'll feel better, and you'll begin to pitch like your old self again. You've got a good pitch, Bernie. It's not unique, but there aren't many guys who can throw it like you can. All you have to do now is forget about that first inning. When you get back out there think of it as a new ball game. Pitch like you pitched the last game and you'll have the Sharks buttering your bread."

The talk melted the lump in Bernie's throat, the heavy feeling in his heart.

He grinned. "Thanks, Coach."

He watched Bill Conley slice at three straight pitches, then walk stiffly to the dugout, his bat on his shoulder.

Ed got a good feel of the ball, driving it out to deep left where Vince pulled it in. Deke cracked the ice by slashing out a single through short, then advancing to second as Buzz walked.

Excitement began to generate on the Ranger bench as Tom got up. He poled two sharp blows just inches outside of the left field foul line, then lined one directly at Vince. Three outs, one hit, no runs. The excitement died.

Bernie again found himself facing the top of the Sharks' batting order. He felt rested, but hardly enough. Nevertheless, with Tim popping up to third, Jess flying out to center, and himself catching a one-hopper that he threw to first for an easy out, he squeezed through the inning.

Rudy fouled two pitches to the back-stop screen, then smashed a hot grounder to third. He was out before he was two-thirds of the way to first.

Chuck laced Luke's first pitch for a long double, then scored on Fred's single through second.

"Okay, Bernie," said the coach. "Let's start a merry-go-round."

Bernie had to practically drag himself out of the dugout. He picked up his bat, stepped to the plate, and eyed Luke's first pitch carefully. It was a ball. So were Luke's next three. Bernie walked.

Bill, after looking over Luke's first two throws – strikes – flied out to left. Ed kept the Rangers alive by driving Fred in with a grass-scorching single through short. But that was it as Deke flied out to center field. 4–2, Sharks.

Bernie felt better as he walked up on the mound to start the first half of the third inning. Vince was up, and again he was smileless, fully determined to powder Bernie's pitch clean out of the county.

He didn't, though. He ticked the first pitch, missed the next, then went down on his fanny as he swung and missed again. The Ranger fans roared.

Bob went down swinging, too, and Sam popped up to first.

"You're in the groove, Bernie!" cried

the coach as Bernie came trotting in. "How do you feel, pal?"

"Much better," Bernie smiled.

Buzz started off the bottom of the third with a triple, finally scoring on Rudy's blazing single through short. Then the combination of good pitching and good fielding on both sides kept the fourth and fifth innings scoreless. The four runs that the Sharks had accumulated in the first inning began to look very big.

As the Rangers came to bat in the bottom of the sixth, Bernie glanced at the stands again for Dave's familiar face. He was sure that if Dave had come to the game he'd be sitting with Frankie. But only AnnMarie was there with him.

Both Chuck and Fred grounded out. One more out, and the victory would go to the Sharks, and the one guy who would never let Bernie forget it would be Vince.

Bernie, at bat, felt that he had never been in a worse spot in his life.

He watched Luke take his stretch, then saw the ball come in, blazing white. He reared back, swung, and *crack!* The ball streaked across the infield and shot past the shortstop for a hit.

The Ranger fans exploded with a tumultuous yell; then Dick, who had replaced Bill in the fourth inning, came to the plate. *Crack!* He connected with a double to left center, and Bernie ran to third where the third base coach held him up.

Arnie Coles, batting for Ed, kept up the spree, scoring Bernie with a single. And so did Deke with a long triple against the right field fence that scored Dick and Arnie. It was over. The Rangers had found the magic touch.

Bernie didn't linger around for the con-

gratulations. He ran to the stands where he met Frankie and AnnMarie coming down.

"Why didn't Dave come?" he asked anxiously.

"We don't know," said AnnMarie. "We wondered that, too."

They hurried home, and Bernie telephoned the Grant residence. The phone rang and rang, but no one answered. Bernie hung up, an ache in his throat. He knew something awful had happened to Dave. He could feel it in his bones.

"Mom," he said, choking back the ache in his throat, "will you call the hospital for me? See if Dave's there?"

She frowned. "You think he might be there?"

He nodded, silent.

"All right," she said.

She made the call. A few seconds later

she replaced the receiver and looked at him. Her hands were trembling. "He's there," she said. "In the intensive care ward."

"Can I see him?" he asked.

"No. Nobody can, except his closest relatives."

Bernie went to his room, took off his uniform, and lay on the bed, praying that Dave would be all right.

An hour later the phone rang, startling Bernie. He was sitting by the living room window, looking out at a bluejay perched on the fence.

His mother answered it. "Bernie," she said, and cleared her voice. "It's for you."

He went to the phone, his legs unsteady, and took the receiver from his mother. "Hello?" he said.

"Bernie, this is Mr. Grant. I wanted to

thank you for calling, but I—I've got some sad news to tell you."

"About . . . Dave?"

"Yes, about Dave," said Mr. Grant. "He has a disease of the liver. I guess he didn't tell you. He never told anybody. He's been fighting a battle with it for the last two years. I hope he's going to get well, but Bernie, he doesn't look too good right now."

Bernie felt his heart split into a million pieces. He choked back tears. "Thanks for calling me, Mr. Grant," he said.

He told the sad news to his family, and when he saw their eyes blink with tears he didn't hold back any longer.

The next morning he went to the hobby shop and bought the model of the *Constitution* that Dave had been saving up for.

He came out of the store and couldn't

believe it when he saw Vince standing there.

"Hi, Bernie," Vince greeted him calmly. "I was coming down the street and saw you go in there. I wanted to apologize about the way I've been acting lately. I guess the track team thing got me down." He paused, then continued. "Too bad about Dave, huh?"

"Yes, it is."

They started to walk down the street together.

"I never knew he was sick, did you?" Vince asked.

"No. He never told anybody. But I suspected that something was wrong with him. He always got tired so quickly."

"He's a great kid. He showed you how to throw that submarine pitch, didn't he?"

Bernie nodded. "He showed me, because he couldn't pitch himself," he said, feeling a lump rising in his throat.

They crossed to the next block.

"Dave was saving to buy this model," said Bernie. "Now that he's so sick, I thought I would for him. I was going to buy a bike, but I figure this model of the *Constitution* is a lot better."

"It sure is a beauty," admitted Vince. "Here, let me carry it for a while. It must be pretty heavy."

"It is," said Bernie, as he handed it over to Vince.

They took turns carrying it as they walked all the way home.

How many of these Matt Christopher sports classics have you read?

Baseball

- ❑ Baseball Pals
- ❑ Catcher with a Glass Arm
- ❑ Challenge at Second Base
- ❑ The Diamond Champs
- ❑ The Fox Steals Home
- ❑ Hard Drive to Short
- ❑ The Kid Who Only Hit Homers
- ❑ Look Who's Playing First Base
- ❑ Miracle at the Plate
- ❑ No Arm in Left Field
- ❑ Shortstop from Tokyo
- ❑ The Submarine Pitch
- ❑ Too Hot to Handle
- ❑ The Year Mom Won the Pennant

Basketball

- ❑ The Basket Counts
- ❑ Johnny Long Legs
- ❑ Long Shot for Paul

Dirt Bike Racing

- ❑ Dirt Bike Racer
- ❑ Dirt Bike Runaway

Football

- ❑ Catch That Pass!
- ❑ The Counterfeit Tackle
- ❑ Football Fugitive
- ❑ The Great Quarterback Switch
- ❑ Tight End
- ❑ Touchdown for Tommy
- ❑ Tough to Tackle

Ice Hockey

- ❑ Face-Off
- ❑ Ice Magic

Soccer

- ❑ Soccer Halfback

Track

- ❑ Run, Billy, Run

All available in paperback from Little, Brown and Company

Join the Matt Christopher Fan Club!

To become an official member of the Matt Christopher Fan Club, send a self-addressed, stamped envelope (10 x 13-inch) to:

Matt Christopher Fan Club
34 Beacon Street
Boston, MA 02108